Dear Parent:
Your child's love of reading starts here!

Every child learns to read in a different way and at his or her own speed. Some go back and forth between reading levels and read favorite books again and again. Others read through each level in order. You can help your young reader improve and become more confident by encouraging his or her own interests and abilities. From books your child reads with you to the first books he or she reads alone, there are I Can Read Books for every stage of reading:

SHARED READING
Basic language, word repetition, and whimsical illustrations, ideal for sharing with your emergent reader

BEGINNING READING
Short sentences, familiar words, and simple concepts for children eager to read on their own

READING WITH HELP
Engaging stories, longer sentences, and language play for developing readers

READING ALONE
Complex plots, challenging vocabulary, and high-interest topics for the independent reader

ADVANCED READING
Short paragraphs, chapters, and exciting themes for the perfect bridge to chapter books

I Can Read Books have introduced children to the joy of reading since 1957. Featuring award-winning authors and illustrators and a fabulous cast of beloved characters, I Can Read Books set the standard for beginning readers.

A lifetime of discovery begins with the magical words "I Can Read!"

Visit www.icanread.com for information
on enriching your child's reading experience.

SPIDER-MAN 3.

MEET THE HEROES AND VILLAINS

Adapted by Harry Lime
Illustrated by Steven E. Gordon
Screenplay by Alvin Sargent
Screen Story by Sam Raimi & Ivan Raimi
ased on the Marvel Comic Book by Stan Lee and Steve Ditko

HarperCollins*Publishers*

COLUMBIA PICTURES PRESENTS A MARVEL STUDIOS/LAURA ZISKIN PRODUCTION A SAM RAIMI FILM TOBEY MAGUIRE "SPIDER-MAN 3" KIRSTEN DUNST JAMES FRANCO THOMAS HADEN CHURCH TOPHER GRACE BRYCE DALLAS HOWARD THEMES BY DANNY ELFMAN SCORE BY CHRISTOPHER YOUNG EXECUTIVE PRODUCERS STAN LEE KEVIN FEIGE JOSEPH M. CARACCIOLO BASED ON THE MARVEL COMIC BOOK BY STAN LEE AND STEVE DITKO

MARVEL SPIDER-MAN CHARACTER TM & © 2006 MARVEL CHARACTERS, INC. ALL RIGHTS RESERVED. SCREEN STORY BY SAM RAIMI & IVAN RAIMI SCREENPLAY BY ALVIN SARGENT PRODUCED BY LAURA ZISKIN AVI ARAD GRANT CURTIS DIRECTED BY SAM RAIMI COLUMBIA PICTURES

sony.com/Spider-Man

Library of Congress catalog card number: 2006934365
ISBN-10: 0-06-083721-7 (pbk.) — ISBN-13: 978-0-06-083721-1 (pbk.)
Book design by Rick Farley and John Sazaklis

❖   First Edition

SPIDER-MAN 3

Everyone is a hero once in a while.

At least I think so.

I always try to do what's right.

But there are bad guys out there, too—

villains.

And that's why I sometimes change
from Peter Parker into someone else.
Who is that other person?
Spider-Man, of course.

When I am Peter Parker,

life is pretty good.

School is fun.

And after school, I like taking photos.

When I am Spider-Man,
I have a lot of work to do!

The life of a super hero isn't easy.

It helps to have good friends.

This is Mary Jane.

She's a great actress.

She works just as hard as I do.

It's not easy to act in plays.

If you want to know the truth,
I like Mary Jane a lot.
I've known her since I was little.
But now she's my girlfriend.

I know Gwen Stacy from school.
We were lab partners.

Gwen wants to be a model.

Her friend Eddie takes pictures
for her.

Gwen's father is Captain Stacy.

He doesn't want her to be a model.

He wants her to stay in school.

Now you've met some of my friends.

But not everyone in this city likes me.

This guy doesn't like me at all.

He is the New Goblin.

He used to be my friend.

But now he is my enemy.

The New Goblin has some cool gear.
He can fly all over the city
on his jet-powered Sky-Stick.

But I am fast, too.

The New Goblin isn't the only bad guy
I have to battle.

There's a new villain in town . . .
Sandman.

andman makes terrible sandstorms.

Sandman needs a lot of money.
And some of the things he does
to get money are really bad!

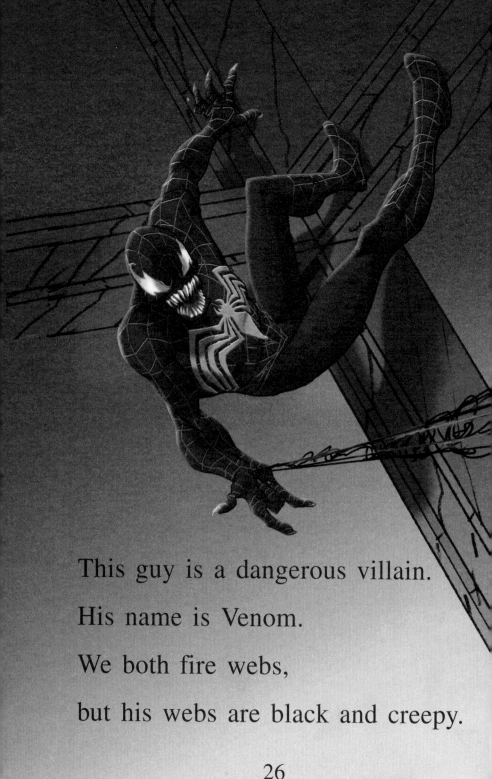

This guy is a dangerous villain.

His name is Venom.

We both fire webs,

but his webs are black and creepy.

Venom is mean to my friends.

And I always stick up for my friends.

29

I like to think there are more heroes
in the world than villains.
A lot of people are my heroes.
And that's a good thing,
because there will always be villains
out there to fight.

And heroes always have to be ready to
do what's right.

When I help people, I feel like a hero.

It feels good.